PANTY

TRANSLATED BY

PANTY

SANGEETA BANDYOPADHYAY

ARUNAVA SINHA

TILTED AXIS PRESS

মন **mōn**

In the ontology that English-reading people have acquired through their books, the heart and the mind are binary - neither word can be used to refer to the other. In Indian languages, however, this word (mōn in Bangla, man in Hindi) represents neither the heart nor the mind exclusively. It takes a position, contextually to the rest of the text, on a continuum between the heart and the mind, between emotion and reason, between feeling and knowing.

- Arunava Sinha

'Ask me no more.'

'But I wanted to know whose lips those were in the darkness.'

'Those lips in the darkness belonged to the kiss.'

'But he didn't kiss me.'

'He didn't?'

'No, he raced away towards deserted Park Street.'

'But I tasted blood on my tongue.'

'Not blood, it was my favourite rum-ball.'

'Not my favourite taste – I always loved the first drops of water drawn from a freshly dug well.'

'But that water was drawn on a January night, when I was deep in sleep, dreaming. The dream ended after fourteen years.'

'Where did that dream of mine end?'

'Beside an earthen pot, on the pavement in front of a teashop. The pot lay there among the broken sherds of many others, lonely. In that spot so dense with rhododendrons it was almost a wood. Although each of the trees had a car parked beneath it.'

'It was raining when the dream ended. So the dream turned into mud. Melting, it flowed to the earthen pot. There was a slatted drain cover close by. A feeble stream of rainwater washed the dream down the drain.'

'That stream came from the city. It contained thousands of newspaper clippings, innumerable stories and novels, a multitude of plays and travelogues. And each of the travelogues ended up in the drain. Who knows whether that isn't where the journey actually begins.'

'I was about to pass by, ignoring this stream. But, at that precise moment, a woman about my age leapt from the roof of a building. She writhed briefly after the impact, then died. A man came running down the stairs. Screaming, "What have you done, what have you done, didn't you even think of the child?" the man flung himself on the woman.'

'At once I made the death my own. "This is my death," I said. I seemed to have rid myself of a weight I had borne some seven or eight months, and the foot I set down on the pavement felt completely new.'

I entered the apartment at eleven at night, unlocking three padlocks in succession. The flat took up the entire first floor of a tall apartment building. I paused for a few moments after entering, trying to make out my surroundings in the light coming in from the passage outside. I found the switchboard near my left hand. Stepping forward, I turned on all the switches. One after the other. And not a single light came on. But I could tell that a fan had started whirring overhead. Once my eyes had adjusted to the darkness, I found myself standing at one end of a hall. The main road below me had begun to quieten down. The light from the street lamps filtered into the dark hall through large windows, creating an unfocused chiaroscuro that came to my aid. Advancing in this hazy glow, I realised that there were doors running down both sides of the hall. On a whim I turned towards an open door on the left.

The room I entered was a large bedroom, with an ensuite. This time, too, I succeeded in locating the switchboard. I swiftly flicked all the switches on. Still not a single light came on. But this time, too, the ceiling fan began to rotate. I tried to understand the layout of the room. It wasn't empty like the hall; rather, it was crowded with furniture. I found myself standing before a mirror stretching across the wall. The reflection didn't seem to be mine, exactly, but of another, shadowy figure. I touched my hair. Eerily, the reflection did not. I paid no attention. Setting my bag down on the floor, I returned to the hall.

Closing the main door, fumbling at the switch-board until I succeeded in turning the fan off, I went back to the bedroom. I was very tired. The train had arrived seven hours later than scheduled. I'd had to scramble for a taxi to get to the flat and collect the key. He'd been waiting for me here since the afternoon. On calling the station and learning that the train was running late, he'd gone back home for a while, then returned to the flat later in the day. Handing me the key, he expressed his regret that all the restaurants in his club were closed at this late hour; otherwise, he would have taken me to dinner. Thanking him, I told him that I had bought myself a slice of cake at the station. He seemed relieved to hear this, and dropped me off at the gate of the high-rise.

Even in the darkness, I could sense another door on the opposite side of the hall. I went forward and opened it. A cold, moist wind instantly swept into the room. The taxi driver had told me it had drizzled all day.

I stepped out onto the balcony. There were several tall buildings in front of me. Fourteen storeys, sixteen, eighteen, twenty-one – going up would be no problem, but if the building caught fire you'd be trapped, unable to climb down. I hurriedly retreated into the room. All I needed was a shower. Fumbling for the towel in my bag, I pulled it out and went into the bathroom. My eyes gradually adjusted to the darkness. I undressed in the light from the street lamps and turned the shower on. A phone began to ring somewhere close by. It kept ringing, no one answered.

Wringing my hair dry, I returned to the room wrapped in the towel and lay down on the bed, feeling the fresh, soft bedclothes against my body. I was cold but I didn't have the strength even to switch the fan off or shut the balcony door. I remained in bed. I remained awake.

Awake, I saw dawn break. I saw colours. The bedclothes were a light blue. The pillow was a light

blue. Three of the walls were off-white, while the
fourth was a somewhat incongruous brown. As the
darkness lifted, the wardrobe, the couch, the mirror –
all became visible one by one. An ancient, radiant
sunlight fell on my bed now. Which meant there was
no rain any more. The towel had come loose long
ago. As I lay there, the sun rose on my nakedness. By
the time I got out of bed, the day was well advanced.
I checked out the kitchen. There were plenty of pots
and pans. It was equipped with a cooking range, a
toaster, a mixer ... everything. In the dining space
was a functioning fridge. I considered exploring the
rest of the flat, but a moment later the desire had
vanished. All I needed was a room.

A phone began to ring somewhere in the hall,
startling me. The sound was just like last night's.
Following the sound to its source, I discovered the
white handset and picked up the receiver.

'Hello?'

'I called last night to check if everything's okay.
Everything's all right, isn't it? I gave my man a list
of the things you might need. I hope you've found
them all.'

The gentleman's voice was courteous.

'Oh yes, I've got everything, thank you so much. I
was in the shower when you called last night.'

'I see. I hope the bathroom's clean.'

'Perfectly clean.'

'Check whether the iron's working. You won't be able to do without an iron.'

'You're right. I'll check.'

'Okay. See you, bye.'

Oh! I didn't tell him about the lights, I remembered after putting the receiver down. The flat was fully equipped, but it didn't have a single working light.

The phone rang again. It was him. 'Should I call your friend and tell her you've settled down?'

'Please, no. There's no need to tell her anything. I … I want to be lost to everyone forever. Just tell her I've arrived.'

He was silent for a few minutes. Then he said, 'You don't have any clothes or anything. How will you manage?'

'I'll buy some soon.'

'Okay then.'

'Excuse me …'

'Yes?'

'How long am I allowed to stay in this flat?'

'As long as you like, more or less.' He laughed. 'Unless something comes up and I need it.'

'Won't your family object?'

'Object? Why should my children concern them-selves with a mere flat?'

'And your wife? Most people wouldn't take it well if you allowed a woman you don't know to stay in a flat belonging to you.'

'Wife? I don't have a wife any more.'

'Do you mean ...'

'She is dead.'

The lights were on my mind throughout this round of conversation. But I didn't bring them up. Heaven knows why. After a shower, I went down into the street. Kolkata! I spent the whole day roaming this unknown city, in taxis, on foot, on the metro. I watched a movie then had dinner at a restaurant, and by the time I got back to the flat it was eleven o'clock. Unlocking the three padlocks one after the other, I entered the unlit interior. Then, allowing my eyes to adjust to the darkness, I slumped on to the dark bed and lay on it the same way I had the previous night. Once again I remained awake. The next morning I opened my bag. I took out the few clothes I possessed and arranged them in the wardrobe. The wardrobe was completely empty except for a single hanger. It would be useful to hang up my trousers, I thought. And in that moment, I caught sight of the crumpled panty.

I picked it up. Imported. Soft. Leopard print. At once I wanted to know who the owner was. Many years ago I had found a blue bangle in a bedside drawer in a hotel room. When I took it in my hand, it seemed to be dripping blue water. That day, too, I'd felt an urge to find out who the owner was.

The panty gave off the smell of moist earth. I saw a white stain on it, like mould. A stain like this in a woman's panty could mean only one thing.

I wondered what to do with the panty. Strangely, I felt a pang of regret at the thought of throwing it away. The panty seemed to offer itself as a second presence in this solitary place. A feeling of companionship.

I didn't throw it away. I tossed it on to one of the lower shelves in the wardrobe. Then I went to the bathroom and washed my hands with soap. I took my documents out of my bag, filed them away, and decided to take care of the phone call before anything else.

'When can I meet you? I'll need your letter.'

'The letter is ready. You can take it today.'

As I dressed after a shower, I chided myself for not remembering about the lights today either. I left the flat again and went down into the streets. After a couple of meetings, I ate a light meal at a restaurant. I bought a loose gown to wear at home. The nakedness of the past two days would finally come to an end.

I met him in the veranda of his club at eight that night. He was poring over a Bengali book, marking up certain passages and scribbling notes in the margins. He also had a Bengali-to-English dictionary by his side. 'So you can read Bengali?', I asked. He nodded, smiling. 'I read it very well.' After accepting the letter from him and sharing some soup and bread rolls, I left him, returning to the flat late at night and unlocking the three padlocks again. I was lying in bed when I felt a certain familiar discomfort, and when I went into the bathroom I discovered that it was just as I had suspected – quietly, my period had started. And my panty was soaked with blood. I had no sanitary napkins. What was I to do, now, at midnight? I didn't have a second pair of panties. I should have thought to pick up a few more things when I was buying the gown. Unless I changed the panty I was wearing, even sitting down would prove impossible, let alone sleeping in the bed. Going by my body's usual routine, the bleeding would intensify in two or three hours. How would I stem this flow of blood? Would any of the shops still be open? If only I could at least get hold of some sanitary napkins …

When I went out to the balcony, wondering what to do, I discovered that there was in fact a pharmacy still open, called Park Medicine, just across the road.

Other than the occasional car speeding by, the roads were deserted. The streets were now under the control of dogs. So many dogs?

Slipping the black trousers back on with a sense of revulsion, I took the lift down and got the durwan to open the gate. I'll only be a minute, I told him. I'm just going to buy some medicine. The first thing I did after getting the sanitary napkins was enter the toilet. With only the glow of the streetlamps to see by, I could still tell that my panty was a mess. Would any shop selling undergarments open before ten o'clock tomorrow morning? How would I tolerate this pair all night? I couldn't bear the thought of having to set fresh sanitary napkins inside the blood-soaked panty. I had to buy a bulb tomorrow and get some light in the bathroom at least. In the morning I'd noticed that there were no bulbs in any of the sockets. Why had the bulbs all been removed? I tried to hold all of this in my mind as I stood there, drops of blood trickling down my thighs into the darkness.

I stood beneath the shower, miserable, while the cold water pounced on me. And then I remembered the black-and-yellow panty I'd found in the wardrobe.

It was a panty worn by someone else, and mouldy to boot — I simply couldn't use it, could I? Who knew whom it belonged to and how long it had lain there that way? A woman who wears a leopard-print panty must be quite wild. At least when it comes to sex. The question was, how wild? Wilder than me, or less so? As these thoughts ran through my mind, I wasn't even aware of having taken off my blood-soaked panty and begun to wring and knead it clean beneath the tap. I stood in bewilderment for some time when I realised what I was doing; eventually I washed it thoroughly and spread it out to dry on the towel rod. I persuaded myself that I had no option now but to put on the other panty. I wasn't going to come in direct contact with the mould, I rationalised. The sanitary napkin would form a layer in between.

Towelling myself dry, I returned to the bedroom and groped for the panty in the dark. I found it, picked up the sanitary napkin I'd laid out on the bed, then paused for a moment before fitting it inside the panty.

I slipped into the panty.

What I did not know was that I had actually stepped into a woman.

I slipped into her womanhood.

Her sexuality, her love.

I slipped into her desire, her sinful adultery, her humiliation and sorrow, her shame and loathing. I had entered her life, though I didn't know it. I even slipped into her defeat and her withdrawal. I slipped into her nation, too, in that moment. Trite thoughts about her world passed through my mind. How fine the material was, I reflected. Soft. A perfect fit. As though tailored especially for me. After putting it on, I was no longer repulsed. I lay down, spreading my hair out on the pillow. Although I do not admit that I fell asleep, it is undeniable that I was woken up by a series of sounds in the room.

They were making out. Kissing. Fucking wildly. They were panting, but could not stop. Hours seemed to pass this way. They remained engaged in their sex – till I passed out.

I had not understood them that first night. I had opened my eyes at the sounds of passion and felt afraid – who were these people in the bedroom! But they weren't in the room – they were on the wall. The one which was painted dark brown. Both of them were on that wall whose colour did not match the rest – naked, having sex, delirious, tearful.

Gradually I realised that they appeared on the days when I wore that particular panty. The leopard-print panty. I heard the woman say, 'If only the past, present and future would pass while we two were conjoined, if only time would just waste away ...' When I heard this desire articulated, I felt as though the big, bigger, biggest expectations whirling restlessly within my vagina had died. So I could not be in pursuit of life any more. A disease had been born within me. My road was gradually coming to an end ...

The days passed without form or shape. When one day ended, I couldn't remember quite how I'd spent it – in what meaningful activities, and in what meaningless ones. Before midnight, I would forget all that had happened throughout that entire day.

I never did get round to buying a bulb.

I didn't even get round to buying a panty.

At times I found the two of them unbearable. I wished they would put an end to it ... but they didn't. Their lovemaking went on and on. In desperation I would pull off the panty and fling it out onto the balcony. Then they would disappear at once.

In the mornings I made tea in the small kitchen. As I sipped my tea, I would feel the pangs starting up again. Strolling out to the balcony, I would pick up the panty and put it back in the wardrobe. The panty definitely smelled of me by then. Of me. How strange!

15

One day I feel a sudden burst of love. It is only after living here all this time that this feeling strikes me. Every day I see how they survive. As I watch them, I realise that I cannot blame the country or the government. For they are always lying down. In dangerous positions.

They sleep. Whenever I look, at least three of the four are asleep. The fourth sits, limbs splayed, with a blank stare. All they do by way of movement is scratch their heads, pick their noses, and spit.

In fact, I never see them eating. Some time after midnight, when the restaurant next door draws down its shutters, the first thing the waiters do is carry out a huge bucket full of the remnants of various delicacies and empty it into a dustbin near the section of pavement where the family live. A pack of dogs immediately throws itself at the leftovers. The three who have been sleeping sit up then. Soon afterwards, someone from the restaurant hands out polythene bags of food, quite a decent amount. That is the only time I ever see them eat.

I don't know where they've come from. I don't know why they have no home. There is such a vast wasteland in and around villages, which no one owns – why don't they go there and build houses for themselves? Why do they languish in this blind city? Why do they linger on the pavement? What attraction does this place hold for them? Why have these two healthy young men been unable to obtain even one of those dark, dank, three-by-four rooms of mud and bamboo in some slum or other?

I don't know where they go during the rains. When it rains at night, I go out on to the balcony – to look for them. But I never manage to spot them. Like the cockroaches that swarm into bathrooms under cover of darkness but disappear the moment the light is switched on, these people vanish into thin air as soon as it starts raining.

Their body language makes it clear they aren't rural folk. They are not people who, overcome by flood or famine, have abandoned a plot of land, or fled their arid farms – house, cowshed, temple, evening gatherings, village plays – in terror, bundling up a few paltry belongings and finally taking sanctuary as penniless beggars here on this pavement. I wonder whether they even are beggars – I have never seen them beg.

They are quite detached from things. Under the open sky, this detachment is fitting. They sleep, wake, eat and rinse their mouths unselfconsciously beneath the krishnachura tree on the pavement. They make love there too. I don't know how they find any privacy, given that every nook and cranny of the deserted road is visible in the light from the tall street lamps. The pavement was empty when I moved into the flat. They came some time later. The wife had a two-month-old baby girl in her arms. And before the year was out, she was holding a ten-day-old infant. There is no doubt that they have sex right there on the pavement.

But it isn't as though they have no possessions at all. They own plates, bowls and polythene sheets. They have blankets for winter, they light coils of mosquito repellent when they sleep. They also have a small gadget to listen to music; I've seen it. I believe they have other belongings too, all neatly arranged in a wooden packing case.

The group consists of two men, about twenty-two or twenty-three, a boy of eleven or twelve, and the woman – between sixteen and twenty – plus the two babies. I have often seen another young man and woman, about the same age, visiting them. I've learned from their conversations that one of the two men is the woman's husband, and the other her brother. I have never seen signs of suffering on their faces. I don't think they have any regrets. They don't think of this form of existence as a failure. This is the way I see them, day after day – the man sleeping, the woman sitting with her legs stretched out before her, leaning against a tree, a distant look in her eyes. The daughter, about a year old now, parts her mother's dirty, tattered blouse to fasten her mouth to her emaciated breast. The mother doesn't even seem to feel the contact. Her expression is dense, exhausted, dispassionate. The very next moment the baby might crawl to the edge of the pavement where the mouth of the drain yawns wide without a lid to cover it. The child may fall in at any moment, but she doesn't. A lively, restive baby might have pitched headlong into the stream of moving cars a couple of feet away. But she's frail; she doesn't scream or cry, doesn't demand food. All she does is sleep. When she wakes, she gropes for her mother's breast. And crawls back without fail from the edge of the pavement, back to her mother.

Only once did I wake up in the middle of the night to the sound of the woman's sobs. I went out to the balcony. I saw the woman rolling on the ground and the man who was her husband raining kicks on her back. The woman's brother, short, squat and well built, was not exactly stopping him. He was only pleading, 'Let her go, she won't do it again.'

'Ask the bitch why she won't let me do it,' said the husband.

'You can see she's pregnant,' said the brother. 'Don't hit her. What'll you do with the baby if she dies?'

The woman, who had been passively allowing the man to hit her all this while, flared up. 'Let him kick me, let the bastard kill me!'

I looked on in astonishment. Why wasn't she trying to defend herself?

'There, her water's broken, leave her alone, leave her alone,' screamed the brother.

Flinging the piece of wood in his hand at the woman's head, the husband disappeared into the darkness. And, to my surprise, the brother ran off in the same direction. After some time, he succeeded in coaxing the husband back to the pavement. The woman was still groaning. I clearly heard the brother say, 'Why did you lose your head all of a sudden? Just look at the state she's in. Have a little patience. And then you'll have a lovely family. You already have a daughter, now if you have a son you can announce it with pride, I have one son and one daughter. What more can you ask for? Show me a person here who's happier than you are.' He began to point at all the air-conditioned high-rises in this plush neighbour-hood, with their dim lights and closed windows. I darted back into the room before he could point at me.

That same night I had a dream. In this dream, nothing else existed from one end of the city to the other but the taut lines of pavements. No houses, no buildings, no shops, no Victoria Memorial, no metro or other transportation – only miles of concrete pave-ments, coiled like a gigantic reptile. Earth's climate had also changed. The air had acquired colour, a shade of red. Like a transparent red scarf floating over everything. And the sun was red too. How peaceful the pavements looked in this red hue.

This is how it has been all these days – but suddenly I feel a burst of affection. When …

When the woman has another child. She begins to nurse the baby in her arms. And I see the one-year-old child lying face down on the ground, heaving with tears. Only heaving. That's it, no other form of protest. Because every time she has approached her mother's breast, her mother has pushed her away. Slapped her. So the girl is weeping. Her lips are puffy, wet with saliva. The weight of unhappiness in her tiny breast is evident.

I didn't know that I would want to go beyond my role as a bystander. I don't hold the state or the government responsible. I don't even consider the family's situation to be particularly dismal. Because I know they sleep all day. Because I know that those who eat and those who don't will both die. But I didn't know how lovely the older child would look when, bent over her rice, she raised her head and glanced up at me, lovely enough for me to feel jealous.

I stuff a polythene bag with a little rice, boiled eggs and salt, and then cross the bedroom to go out on to the balcony. When I catch a glimpse of myself in the mirror, I find my wings have fallen off, the backache is gone too.

I forge a relationship with them – for the first time. Actually, my relationship with you had also flowered by then. In fact, by then I had already told you, 'I want to live with you.'

She was walking. Along an almost silent lane in the city.

Work – she had abandoned her work a long time ago, to walk. The sky had just turned a happy black.

As she walked, she mulled over two words – 'legitimate' and 'illicit'. The presumption that these words were innate opposites – how totally were individuals expected to acquiesce to this! And yet the illicit held the greatest attraction for all that was legitimate.

Once, in an urge to ascertain the meanings of 'legitimate' and 'illicit', she had wished for a space that was at once one of emptiness and of equilibrium, the kind of space that defied the laws of nature. She had searched for such a space, but never found it.

Having walked for hours, when she came to her senses she discovered herself in the lane she was in now. And saw that the place was unfamiliar.

The lane was narrow and deserted, with ramshackle houses on either side. The bricks were exposed in the crumbling walls. The windowpanes were broken, and dirty water dripped from the pipes. Sucking out all the life force from this water, a banyan sapling had begun to rear its head. There were three or four antennae on the roof of every house in this lane full of potholes and crevices. Thousands of crows sat on the antennas. So many crows that the city would turn dark if they were all to spread their wings simultaneously.

Only a handful of rickshaws rattled by, some pulled by hand, some with pedals. There was the odd passer-by, humming, cigarette tip glowing. A dog whined at the sight of one of them. She was about mid-way down the lane when it was abruptly plunged into impenetrable darkness. A power cut had swooped down like a black panther, gobbling up the lane. Everything was annihilated by the killer paw of darkness.

She couldn't decide what to do. Carry on? Go back? Both options appeared equally futile. She sensed the blindness even within her consciousness.

Surprised by her awareness of the extreme silence all round, a strange touch against her lips caused her to jump out of her skin.

Someone's lips descended on hers; on the lips alone. They didn't touch her anywhere else, the rest of her remained untouched and absolutely free; in the utter darkness an unknown pair of lips kissed hers deeply. A mild pain of being bitten and mauled, the warmth, the saliva, and the fire of an unfamiliar ache spread across her lips as one.

A kiss! A kiss! A kiss! She felt the kiss right down to its roots. So this was a kiss? So this was a kiss, when it was detached from the rest of the body? When – completely dissociated from the heart, from the consciousness, from even the obstacle of knowledge – a pair of lips united with another? When it was the coming together only of two pairs of lips? An isolated union?

In that darkness, the disembodied lips filled her lips, her tongue and the fleshy cavity of her mouth with the taste of the kiss, and she stood erect, savouring this novel feeling. She was hooked. When the lips left her, ending the kiss, the first sensation that returned was of sound. She heard, in turn, the sound of metal being hammered, of bus wheels rotating, of anklets jingling in a nearby house. The street lamps snapped back on, and the movement of people resumed. A dog howled.

She wanted to cry. She stood there for a long time, pressing her fingers to her lips. All this time, she'd thought she knew what a kiss was. Just as she'd thought she knew what love was, what the body was, what art was. When in fact she had known none of these.

She resumed her slow walk to the bottom of the lane. And then, as she turned the corner onto the main road, the meaning of 'illicit' became clear to her.

She had returned to the same lane many times since then, always just as dusk descended. There she would stand still and wait for the lights to go out, for a kiss to swoop down on her.

I would have left. But the plants flourished so beautifully in the rains that I couldn't bear to part from them. The very evening you told me to leave, I bought a casuarina with slender, shimmering leaves.

'Did you really mean what you said?' you asked.

I looked at the fountain. There was no one else on the veranda of the club. 'Yes,' I said.

You downed your vodka in a single gulp.

'If that's what you think,' you said, 'then promise me you'll leave.'

I turned my gaze to you.

'You'll need a week or so to recover from your surgery, you can wait until after that.'

'Yes,' I said.

'It's a deal ...' You held out your hand.

'It's a deal,' I repeated, extending my hand as well. I found your hand excessively cold. Unable to accept my touch.

'There's no need to discuss it any further,' you said.

'Very well,' I responded.

'Come, let's go.' Taking the car keys from the table, you crossed the hall and headed towards the portico. I followed you. There was still quite a crowd in the hall. Many of them waved to us, bidding us good night. 'Leaving?' some asked. I nodded, smiling, at the familiar faces. 'Staying or leaving are actually distinct decisions,' I said to myself.

The word 'decision' immediately reminded me of a particular conversation we'd had, a long one, over tea at your friend's house. Your friend said, 'This has happened to me many times, you know. I can't see what lies ahead. Everything seems to be shrouded in mist. Should I advance or retreat? Or perhaps I'm standing at a fork in the road. Two or more paths lie ahead. But I can't decide which one to choose.'

You said, 'Your soul will tell you which road to take. You will hear your soul direct you.'

'But very often it isn't clear,' your friend said. 'Personal experience isn't always enough to predict the outcome of a decision. The soul has nothing to help it proceed. So it's confused. What then? How will you decide? Tell me.'

'You have to know yourself inside out,' you told your friend. 'You have to understand what it is you really want. Actually, all our decisions have been taken before our life even begins. We only come to know of each decision when we accept it. We discover that a given decision has in fact been taken already, long before we were even aware of it.'

Your friend's wife put down her cup of tea. Looking at you eagerly, she said, 'Explain.'

'That's not so easy,' you said. 'Probably impossible. All I can do is give you an example. Let's say I'm out driving one day and I run someone over. The decision about what to do with the injured man has already been taken, before my life even began. All that's left to me at that moment is to stand at the confluence of time and feel a mild throbbing in my brain. That's where all the decisions are gathered, waiting to emerge with the flow of events.'

I was sitting beside you in the passenger seat, thinking of that day. As we crossed Elgin Road, you said, 'Take the medicine at night.'

I sighed. 'No, I won't take any more medicine.'

'Don't call me and cry when the pain gets worse.'

'No, I won't cry.'

'I'll put all the phones on silent when I go to bed tonight. I've put up with enough disturbance these past months. No more.'

'Just give me a couple of days, then I'll leave.'

You braked. 'What are you talking about? I told you you can go after the surgery.'

'I'm not going to have the surgery.'

You looked about for the bottle of water. I didn't help you. Unable to locate the bottle, you started the car again. After you dropped me off, you waited a couple of moments before speeding away.

Once inside the flat, I lay down without changing my clothes. I told myself that I would have to find a place very soon. I would have to pack all my things and get ready for the move. I'd accumulated so many belongings over the past year and a half. Just needless baggage, I told myself. I should have kept in mind that I might have to leave at any moment. The biggest question was: Would I find a flat to rent in Kolkata within the time I needed? Would I be able to get a space of my own?

I went out on to the balcony very early the next morning. There was a cool breeze. The city appeared tranquil. I ran my gaze over all the plants on my balcony, studying them. I had so many in my collection now. Some hanging, some in their special pots. Here was someone out for a morning stroll. The city would be awake in another half hour – hundreds of people and vehicles would emerge onto the roads. The noise would build. Clothes washed in the morning would be black by the afternoon, even before they had fully dried. Layers of dust would settle on the plants, rendering them unrecognisable within a matter of days.

But it was the monsoon now and the plants on my balcony were free from any grime. In fact, they were flourishing. Now, at this moment, they seemed so happy to be close to me. All nodding and smiling in the cool breeze.

Was I upset? Was I upset at the thought of having to leave these plants? Would I find a house in the next two days with space for them, these glowing plants that had been reborn in the rains? If not, would I abandon them, leaving them to die for lack of water after the rains ended? Or should I tell the durwan to take them away? All they needed to stay alive was a little water at the end of each day, nothing more.

How many things could I possibly pack into the next two days? Look for a flat, pack up my belongings, make arrangements for the plants … Would I be able to get it all done?

The white kochupata plant was dying. I had revived it with great effort. Five of its leaves were now fully open, with another one halfway there. If this sixth leaf managed to unfold, I'd know for sure that the plant was completely healthy. Would it happen within the next two days?

The vendor had said that blue flowers would bloom all year round on the hanging vine. Were year-round flowers just a dream? Would I have to leave before the flowers bloomed? Impossible!

No, I couldn't leave in two days. I wouldn't. The phone rang in the hall. Who else could it be so early in the morning but you? Who else do I know in this city, anyway? I turned to answer the phone, walking towards it slowly.

'It's absolutely no use being angry with you. It's stupid,' you said. You laughed. You didn't sleep at all last night, did you? Instead, you thought of me, didn't you? You wanted to call, you didn't want to call. You battled with yourself – I could tell.

'What are you trying to say?' I asked. I laughed. I hadn't slept last night either. Instead, I'd thought of you. I'd wanted to leave, but I had to change my decision for the sake of the plants. For the sake of the plants.

'Have you taken your medicine?'

'Yes. I think I have a fever, my eyes are smarting. My whole body aches.'

'I'm calling the doctor right away …'

'No, let it be … I'll be fine.'

'Are you mad? Haven't you heard about this viral fever going round? Listen, let's take a break after your surgery. We could go to the jungle … or the hills? It's been a long time.'

'For how long?'

'A month, say?'

'So long?'

'Why not?'

'What about my plants?'

'What? I can't hear you properly, the line's bad …'

'All right, I'll put the plants out in the passage. I'll tell the durwan to water them every day.'

'What?'

'Nothing.'

'Listen, you wouldn't have said what you said yesterday if that wasn't how you really felt. But I'm not angry now. What's the use of being angry with you, anyway? I can't live without you, after all. It's not possible any more.'

'Actually, the decisions about whether to go or not to go, to live without someone or not to live without someone, have all been made long ago, at a time when we weren't even aware that they existed. Only when confronted with a given situation do we get to find out what the decision was …'

'What the hell are you talking about, woman? Try to get some sleep now. I'll ask the doctor to drop by later, okay?'

'You're not angry, are you? Angry enough to go away?'

'Don't worry. The plants alone are enough to keep me here. And anyway, how far can anger really drive you? Yes, you might get angry, but you still stay on …'

One overcast dawn she stood before a mass of water. A sprawling, mysterious, complex body of water. A row of trees where the water ended. A capricious sky overhead. Geese flying over a rusting crane, half-submerged near the water's edge. She tried to absorb this entire scene into her senses, fervently – and without applying rationality. Absolutely without rationality.

She noticed some sort of disturbance in the distance, in the water at the far side. Narrowing her eyes, she tried to ascertain the cause of the ripples.

After a few moments she could make out someone in the water, swimming in her general direction. Actually towards her?

The body was mostly concealed, though. She could see only two sturdy arms, rising and falling. The same movement was repeated in quick succession, rhythmically, as though the man was in the grip of an acute compulsion. His arms glistened in the sunlight, his muscles flashed.

She felt strangely aroused, a forbidden warmth spreading to the hidden parts of her body, a sensation more primal than the numerous experiences of her past.

The concealed body drew nearer, surfacing in stages.

She shut her eyes.

When she shut her eyes, did she fall asleep?

Did she imagine the whole thing?

The man emerged from the water and the eternal, unquestioning game between man and woman instantly began anew, creating two opposing but complementary forces. Which, if generated with integrity, would eventually leave behind on the grass the principles of pure sexuality, principles in which you had tried to educate her, but which she had been prevented from understanding – prevented by fear, and nothing else.

1

She had stayed up all night. Hadn't she also stayed up all day? Waiting. Waiting to write the rest. In fact, she hadn't written anything for months. She'd done nothing but practise walking. Walking far, far away, and then returning, still on foot, from that far, far away.

With great effort, she'd managed to get hold of a bag. From then on, she'd started to gather paper while she walked. She gathered paper, and put it in her bag. She walked. In this way, she'd managed to write – but only a single line. She would be able to sleep as soon as she had written the second line. Sleep during the day, sleep at night. But even after all her walking, she hadn't found her second line.

So was this solitary line the only thing she would ever write? Was this one line all the blood that would ever flow from the wounds?

She continued walking. When her bag was full of paper, she went to the riverbank. Perhaps the sun was setting then. She emptied her bag into the water. She tried to tell herself that she loved this water, that this star was her favourite, that this wandering death was the outcome of her ambition. This disease, this defencelessness – that this was actually what enabled her to live, to survive.

And she tried to tell herself that not writing could achieve more than writing could. The wounded pride of the solitary line she had written touched her. For on one side of this line lay one eternity, while on the other side lay eternal time. In the process of writing the line, she had introduced a deathlike silence into it. The line had died despite all its possibilities. The possibility of creating something from out of creation. The possibility of life emerging from life.

'Weep,' the river had told her. And the moment you did, you thought of him. You thought of how long it had been since you last saw him. A long time. The way things happen after a break-up. 'Maybe we'll meet again after we die,' you had said.

Believing that she had found her final or second line, she postponed her tears and began to run. And realised this was how it was, this was the poet's life. The poet's manuscript was made up of all these suppressed tears. The failure of tears. The poet did not weep for herself, nor for others. The poet wept only for poetry.

What use was writing? None at all. The world had seen so much of it, but no one had found it to be of any practical use. Or, no one bothered to make use of it. They'd simply read the words, then forgotten them.

She too had asked herself when writing each new word, 'What have you just written? The words have vanished behind the tree.' Besieged with doubt, she stopped writing.

Then night fell. And the worms in her head began to wriggle. Trying to crawl out through her eyes and ears and nose and mouth. The look in her eyes changed. There was a toxic vapour in her breath; she heard obscene words muttered, uttered some herself. And writhed on the floor. Eventually, she quietened down, twisting her scarf as she watched the whirling fan. Like a hangman, she practised making a noose.

Then someone pushed her back to writing. Trembling, she wrote. Writing, she slept. This is release, she thought.

This newspaper at the start of the day. Every page that touched her sleep-hazed skin bore pictures of burnt bodies. She felt miserable, distracted. Grief flowed easily through her slack limbs.

All these children had burnt to death at a school in Tamil Nadu. They had held one another as they burned. As though that had helped, somehow, to mitigate the agony. As though they were telling us that if we ever got the chance to burn to death as a collective, we too should hold one another.

At first it was rumoured that several teachers had died along with the children. But with the passage of time it was revealed that no, none of them had died. They had managed to escape in time. Eighty children had died, all aged seven or eight. Many more were in the state general hospital, expected to die very soon.

A photograph in an English-language daily brought her to her knees. A Tamil father was weeping, holding in his arms a blackened piece of wood. It was his child … No, this was too much so early in the morning.

Quickly folding the papers, she threw them into the bedroom. She switched on the microwave to make herself some tea. She wanted to escape from the news. Instead, she found herself trapped, helpless, in the time between the beginning of the fire and its being put out – the time in which those eighty, ninety, one hundred children had burned to death – and stood stock still, picturing the flames licking at her own skin, flesh and bone marrow, while the water for the tea boiled away into steam.

Then she went to have a shower to allay her agony and wept, heaving, in a terrible rage.

The phone rang. She stepped out of the shower, wrapped herself in a towel and went to answer it. She explained that she'd just been in the shower. Yes, she had been naked. Yes, she had soaped herself. Yes, she would soap herself again with you in mind and, fingering herself, say exactly three times – 'I'm yours, I'm yours, I'm yours.' She would need ten minutes more to get dressed. You could leave now, and in the meantime she would finish showering, get dressed, then come downstairs to wait for you. Yes, you were coming over to take her out shopping, for all the things to turn the flat into a home. A house, a householder, a home. That's what you wanted. 'Make yourself at home.'

She went back to finish her shower. Afterwards, she put on the clothes she'd set out. Combed her hair. Sprayed herself with perfume. Went downstairs. You picked her up.

She was out the whole day, buying all manner of things. The two of you had dinner, then she returned to the flat. Unlocked the padlocks one by one and went straight into the bedroom.

When she switched on the light, the morning's newspapers were there on the bed. The photographs on each front page seemed to come alive when they saw her. Shrinking back, she burned in those flames, the fire that rages at the circumference of life, engulfing the escape route.

The phone was ringing. It was you, calling to tell her to 'go to sleep'. She answered, 'I had a son, he was six. One day there was a fire in our high-rise. On an afternoon when I was far away, lying beneath a man I barely knew. My son was alone with the live-in maid – his father was also far away. When the girl became aware of the fire she fled, leaving the boy behind. He called me on my mobile and told me what was happening. The floor beneath his feet had become very hot, he said. The flames had come into the room through the windows, shattering the glass. He was coughing, choking. But I could still hear the hurt in his voice as he asked, "Why did you go away, Maa, why did you leave me?" Then I heard an explosion. That was all. There was no other sound after that, only the crackling of the flames …'

You said nothing. She was the one to break the silence. 'I ran away. I escaped to the centre, inside the fire that rages at the circumference of life.'

The foreign woman is pinching the girl's cheeks. She has leaned over so far that her long skirt is sweeping the ground. They give her a battery case to sit on. I step back inside, off the balcony.

The foreign woman is still there when I go back out. She is sitting on the battery case. And the family are sitting around her, on the pavement. The little girl stands on tottering legs, staring at the foreign woman in astonishment. She really is worth staring at. The sunlight is blinding on her white skin. Both the skirt and top she has on are white. A multicoloured Jaipur scarf is draped around her throat. Perfect proportions, strong build. She might be German. Her shining red hair is piled high on her head. A Rajasthani sling bag hangs from her shoulder, covered in shells and tiny mirrors.

She is explaining something to the woman, waving her hands. She takes the little girl in her arms. Lighting a cigarette, she offers it to the woman's husband. She kisses the little girl's filthy cheek.

A few days ago, standing on that part of the pavement while I waited to cross the road, I'd noticed that the little girl's ears and nose had been pierced. It made me recoil in horror. What kind of unreasonable behaviour was this? How it must have hurt – now, she won't even allow her mother to wipe her nose. It must still be hurting. I watch the foreign woman take tissues out of her bag to lovingly wipe the dark green mucus streaming down towards the child's lips.

It appears that she is making the family a proposition, one which they aren't quite willing to accept. The husband and wife smile doubtfully at each other.

I'm worried that the foreign woman wants to take the child away. I cannot guess how or on what conditions she plans to do it. But I realise I reek of burnt flesh. The scene appears incredibly vulgar. I come away.

The child has grown quite a lot over the past few months. However filthy she might be, one look at her plump fists and you want to cuddle her. Her smile is just like the fronds on her flower-print dress. When I go downstairs, she catches sight of me and ducks behind the tree. Then she peeps out, smiling shyly. But when I go up to her, she looks away, trying not to smile. I'm surprised at the way her eyes sparkle with intelligence. At such times I long to take her away, to teach her to read and write. To give her a full meal. To give her brushes and paints. To teach her Rabindranath's songs …

Even after leaving the balcony I fret. What's going on? What does the foreign woman want?

I bring the child food every day. Do I think that this gives me a claim on her? Why am I feeling so restless otherwise? If what I fear comes true, if the foreign woman does take her away and bring her up as her own, I should be happy that the girl has been given an opportunity for a decent human existence.

For I know very well that my involvement is partial. None of this child's needs are fulfilled by it. Will I ever be able to risk anything more for her than a single square meal a day?

Although this truth has staked its claim over my mind, it cannot touch my heart. Instead, I feel sobs welling up in my throat. My agitation grows. I glance at the clock, pack the rice and boiled egg in the polythene packet and go downstairs. I look as arrogant as the midday sun.

I stand at an angle to the mother of the child and the foreign woman, who says 'Hi' to me. But the mother doesn't even acknowledge my existence. She stretches out her hand for the packet and hangs it up on the tree. When I take a couple of steps towards the child, she runs to her mother, burying herself in her mother's breast.

I hurry back to the building, jabbing impatiently at the lift button. I call you. Choking with tears, I pound the table. 'No more food for her. No more. I'm telling you, no more food for her.'

I stop bringing her food after that. The days pass one by one. She doesn't go anywhere. The foreign woman doesn't come and whisk her away to some sheltered, affluent life, cosseted and secure. Sleeping, her fist lies in the pavement's dust, and passers-by step over it with ease.

I go out onto the balcony when the sun is overhead. I check whether her mother looks up at me expectantly.

No, she does not. Instead, it is I who keep on stealing glances. And dream that the child is lying on the end of my sari, in the veranda of a thatched hut, on a green plot of land very far away from here. Silvery water hugs a moonlit sandbank. A pot of rice is boiling in the corner of a scrubbed-clean court-yard. Our sleep deepens amid the fragrance of rice, of potato, of lime. The pain that covers the length and breadth of the world is obliterated.

19

She called you, wanting to tell you about the pain. Though she had her doubts about whether it could be called a pain.

There was a strike in the city, a bandh. There was no need to get out of bed in the morning. But she had risen early, disturbed by the sensation of pain. Pain, in the sense of a hive of discomfort centred on a single nipple.

The uneasiness had begun with a tingling sensation at the tip of her right nipple. It intensified gradually. She began to scratch the place with her left hand, small scratches with her fingernail, and realised that the tip of a nipple was completely different from the rest of the body. It was made so that it could not be scratched. Doing anything to this tiny piece of wrinkled flesh only meant hurting it further. Rubbing it with a piece of cloth had provided some comfort, though, its brown areola becoming swollen and warm.

She even massaged it with a little olive oil, but to no effect.

She'd suddenly thought of your teeth. Surely, she thought, they would bring some relief. Closing her eyes, she had imagined her nipple being cared for in the cavity of your mouth. You were relieving her of her agony, slowly, using the sharpness of your teeth, your saliva, and the warmth of your mouth. She'd called you immediately afterwards.

'I'm in pain,' she said.

'What's wrong?' you asked. 'What kind of pain?'

'I'm very lonely,' she said.

'I know that,' you answered.

She began to speak, in part to herself. 'Yes, I feel lonely. Terribly lonely. This loneliness gripped me in childhood. I lived in a dark house back then, a dark, damp house, like a cave in a hillside. And yet, just outside the cave were human dwellings, full of sounds, ups and downs, sirens, tears, laughter. But a wall of thunder and lightning and rain lay between me and these dwellings, impossible to breach. I imagined that the rain would end at some point and I would be able to run out among the houses, among the people. But that incessant, impenetrable rainfall went on and on. My jaw ached from having no one to talk to. I spent entire days just pacing from one room to another.

Today's strike means there is no dust, so smoke, none of the usual sounds. The emptiness is becoming more palpable. No call from you all morning, no call from you all afternoon. Why not? Was it deliberate?'

'…'

'Didn't you think of me even once?'

'Of course I did.'

'Then why didn't you call?'

'No time.'

'No time? Didn't you shower? Didn't you eat? Did work leave you no time for any of that?'

'Don't quarrel with me, please. I'm tired of quarrelling with you.'

'No, I don't want to quarrel. I only want you close to me.'

'Now? There's a strike. How will I get there?'

'Last time there was a strike you made it just fine.'

'I hadn't let my driver off that day. I don't feel like driving myself. And besides, I had no work that day. Listen to me, please, I've got to hang up now. I was just in the middle of sending an email …'

'No, don't hang up,' she screamed in desperation. 'Don't hang up, talk to me some more. Talk to me. Millions of people all around me, so why am I such a beggar? Have I run out of companionship too? Even my death doesn't draw a crowd, when I imagine it.

No one follows my funeral procession. Not even you. I often run a fever these days, I throw up. This flat turns into a ship from whose deck I stare out alone into the darkness. And sharks come to the surface. Innumerable sharks ... and when the ship strikes an iceberg and sinks, I go through two kinds of death at the same time.'

'Be quiet, be quiet. You've gone mad.'

'I'm not mad at all. I'm waiting to make a home. I've taught myself how to make besan chapattis. I'm even waiting for you to scold me, so loud it makes the windowpanes ring, for all the things I haven't yet learned.'

'You won't get a home from me. I can only give you the life you have now. It's too late for me to give you anything more.'

She fell silent. You said 'Hello? Hello?', a couple of times and then hung up. She broke down in tears, thinking she'd gone mad. And kept saying, 'So I've gone mad now, so I've gone mad now.' She repeated the words in an attempt to prove to herself that she was insane. She decided not to talk to anyone any more. She would not eat, would not sleep, would not even bathe. She would just sit staring at the floor. She knew that you would send her to a lunatic asylum then. You would visit her once or twice. Once or twice, then no more. No one would ask you anything about her because everyone believed that your relationship would sink into the darkness at any moment. This was natural. Or, more likely, no one else was aware that any such relationship existed.

Feeling overcome by complete insanity, she fell to the floor and wept – crawling back into the bedroom. Spittle trickled out of her mouth. The bell rang. The doorbell.

Lunatics don't answer the doorbell, she thought. But she decided it would be best to avoid unnecessary harassment. Lunatics never wipe away their spit, either, but she dried her mouth before opening the door. She assumed that she wouldn't have to look or listen too closely to whoever was there.

When she opens the door you, yes you, step forwards and put your arms around her. She tries to free herself, but that only makes you tighten your grip. 'Really, you do look like you've gone mad,' you say.

'Yes, I have, but I won't go to the asylum,' she answers.

This makes you laugh. 'Asylum? Can your madness ever be cured? Why would the asylum make room for you?'

'Then where do you want to dump me?' she bursts into tears. 'Let's go there, today, right now.'

You crush her to your ribs. 'What is it? Why are you so unhappy?'

Your voice grows moist. You feel her body turning limp in your arms.

You drag her to the bed and make her lie down, realising just how deep your involvement is, your fondness, affection, love and lust. So you kiss her, helplessly. You think of god in your passion. Your lips descend upon hers, then move to her neck. Then, when you remove her clothes and her right breast fills your hand, you see the swollen nipple. You frown, pinching it between two fingers, feeling the intense heat radiating from it. 'What's this? What's happened?' you exclaim.

She lies there with her eyes closed, tears streaming down her face. 'I don't know,' she says. 'I've had a tingling ache since this morning. It's absorbed all the pain that this desolate, shut-off room, this loneliness, can inflict. It's brought a pinpoint of agony to my body, destroying all the numbness.' She thrusts the nipple towards your lips. 'This was why I asked you to come. Because it hurts – and I can't scratch it ...'

Your eyes fill with tears. 'Why didn't you tell me?' you say, as, with great compassion, you fit your mouth to her right nipple and suck out all her suffering.

2 4

━━━━━

In the middle of an afternoon, when a terrible Loo was blowing, and without any thought or consideration, she'd boarded a ramshackle bus. It wasn't exactly crowded, but most of the seats were occupied. She found one that was empty and sat down. Only then did she notice that there were no other women on the bus.

When she also realised that the other passengers all followed a particular religion – something which was apparent from their clothes, beards, shoes, even the rings on their fingers – she was overcome by an unwonted fear. She felt a numbing sensation sweep through her entire body, like pins and needles. She tried to steal a glance at her co-passengers, all men, but fear had blinded her, preventing her from making out their individual features. And the visible signs of this religion, which each seemed compelled to display on their person, began to deeply disturb the humanism she'd maintained all these years. Assailed by feelings of insecurity, she sat ramrod-straight despite the swaying of the bus.

When she turned to look out of the window, a shriek slipped out before she had time to clamp her hand over her mouth. It wasn't just the bus – the entire street seemed to have been engulfed by this other faith. The architecture of the houses and the names of the shops; the array and origins of the products on sale; the men, women and children; the language, music, laughter, movement, gestures, designs, prayers ... all of it sent a single throbbing signal into every crevice of her consciousness, a broadcast from another religion. The bus and the street it was travelling down became a separate world, pushing her deeper into the darkness.

The blood in her veins had been quickened by the knowledge that she was the sole representative of her faith on this bus – much more than by her being the sole woman. Was her religion then a stronger and more primal factor than her womanhood? She'd had no religion when she got on the bus. For she considered religion as something akin to art – both remake that which already exists in natural form. Therefore religion seemed to her to be an artificial compulsion. But as the bus pulled her down the street she felt herself being formally indoctrinated, though she remained aware that she had no personal inclination towards religious beliefs or habits. Still, she did have a connection with one particular religion, a connection that was unconditional, and ran through to the core. But her existence now was free from that period in her past which this religion had invaded. Back then, had it insinuated itself into her identity? But she was attracted to the idea of there being more than one religion. Religion wasn't born of the intellect, it wasn't a pursuit of mōn, and neither was it a particular set of actions, since she herself had never conformed to prescribed behaviour. And yet she had maintained a religious disposition, even without following its instructions. Actually, was religion not simply a memory? A memory of the dreams of past lives.

So, ultimately, she – who had no name, no identity, no family, no city or village, no property or assets – had still retained a religion. A religion acquired without the application of effort, ability, reason or questions. She'd made no effort to hold on to it, and yet, in stark contrast to the ease with which objects slipped from her hand, or relationships from her life, this religion hadn't fallen by the wayside.

While riding the bus, religion felt as natural as her body's nervous reflexes. The bus arrived at a place where everything had changed again – the street name, the shop signs, the religious symbols on women's bodies, the religious practitioner seated beneath a tree, the desire for religion as expressed in food, the search for it in people's expressions. Averting her eyes from the sight of a dog urinating on a broken clay idol, the embodiment of woman worshipped in her own religion, she discovered her fearsome and fear-prone wariness vanishing, and found herself once more able to ignore her religion.

Back in her flat, she considered telling you that secularism is not a credo but a shifting situation, eternally mutable …

In her sleep she recognised the music school from her childhood. She remembered it as having been constantly under construction. A hill took up most of the grounds. Stacks of bricks next to it. Scaling the hill, her small feet slipping down with each step, brought the layers of bricks into view. She often played in the sand, but never ventured too close to the bricks. Fear held her back. For the experiences of her still-brief life had taught her that brick piles were the haunt of snakes.

Now and then she sank up to her waist in the sand. She could feel that the sand inside was damp – it was fun. She rolled down the sandy slopes. When she stood up, sand clung to every uncovered inch of skin. Even once she'd dusted herself down, something glittering remained behind.

She also rummaged for snail and oyster shells in the sand, picking out the largest and smallest to absently clutch on her way home. She planned to show everyone her collection, only she could never remember where she'd put them, and they were usually lost for good after a day or two. In her sleep she saw herself gathering shells. The sun had not set yet. The sunlight glinted strangely on the reddish sand. The sand glittered. She spotted countless shells and busied herself with gathering them. That was when she saw the snake. Its hood was raised.

It was the same colour as the sand; it glittered in just the same way. The snake had also seen her. She was afraid – pressed up against a solid, impenetrable wall of fear. Her skin prickled all over, she looked around in desperation – directly in front was the peak of the sand hill. Behind were the brick piles. To her left, the half-finished music school. There was no one around who could be referred to as 'someone', someone whom she could call on for help. Not that any sound would have emerged from her throat.

The snake was still at a slight distance from her, but it was impossible for her to turn and run, because you couldn't run on sand.

The snake was swaying. She was conscious of it swaying, though she couldn't look at it directly – it was too repulsive. As though her vision had been smeared with something slimy. She looked at the sun, picturing the snake in its entirety. But it was impossible to shut her eyes.

Despite the presence of the snake in this desolate place where there was no one to rescue her, she was too young for the idea of death to present itself. She was only worried about the pain of being bitten. She tried to tighten her grip on the shell she was holding but it slipped out of her perspiring hand, gashing her soft palm as it dropped to the sand. She could feel the blood oozing out but she didn't look down at it, keeping her eyes fixed midway between the sun and the hood of the snake.

She couldn't have said how much time passed this way, but at some point she spotted a man on the sand hill.

Even out of the corner of her eye, she could see what the man was doing. He had taken off his shirt and, after a brief pause, was skilfully using it to whip the snake.

She ran. Trying to drag her feet across the sand instead of sinking into it, she tripped and fell on the brick steps of the music school, and began to cry.

The man appeared a little later at the spot where she sat weeping. Sand clung to his thin body. He had sand in his hair too. Looking at her bleeding palm, he said, 'No poison.' She sobbed loudly.

The man took her right hand, the uninjured one, and led her into the school. The floor had not yet been laid. Just bricks. Brick walls. A hole where the window was supposed to be. The room was dark. The air inside was moist, damp. Outside, the sun had set.

She saw a mosquito net rolled up in a corner of the room. A pitcher of water next to it. A shirt, trousers and a towel hung on the wall. The man had hollow cheeks, sunken eyes and a tangled mop of hair.

She didn't like the man. She tried to free herself from his grip so she could go home, but he kept a firm hold on her, refusing to let go. Now she felt a different kind of fear. An unfamiliar fear, but still she couldn't tell him to let go of her hand. The man rinsed her hand with water from the pitcher, and then made her sit down on the mosquito net. Looking at the hole that was the door, she wondered why she had run towards the school building.

'I want to go home,' she said. The man nodded. Then he pulled a book out from behind the pitcher and handed it to her. She was startled when she looked at it.

There was a picture of a naked girl on the green cover. The book was old and filthy. She dropped the book and tried to run away. But the man's bony hand was like a pincer gripping her arm. She panted and sobbed. The man pushed the book back into her hands.

She opened the book. A group of naked boys and girls, standing, sitting, lying on their backs or stomachs, seemed to come alive in the faint blue light. She realised that they were doing strange things with the places between their legs, and seemed to be calling to everyone to watch them as they did so. Her stomach turned, her heart was hammering, her throat was dry, but she couldn't toss the book aside. Her hands were numb. Even the gash in her left hand no longer hurt. The man beckoned to her, and when she glanced at him, he signalled to her to look lower down. She did. She saw that his trousers were unzipped and that a dark, limp object was poking out. She recognised it right away. A comparison popped into her mind: it looked like a rotten, shrivelled jackfruit that had fallen to the ground. The man shook it a couple of times, and then looked at her.

He glanced alternately at her, the pictures in the book, and the limp thing. His eyes shone in expectation.

She managed to free herself and pelted straight out of the room. She looked back over her shoulder without slowing down. No, there was no one chasing her.

She never told anyone about this. Not about the snake, not about the man. She never went back to the music school. In fact, it was a long time before she would even leave the house. But she saw the man. She saw him standing under a drumstick tree a little way off, peering into a book. A book with a green cover. Or passing by her house, again with the book in his hands.

Tossing in her sleep, she reflected that for a long time she would see a dry, shrivelled jackfruit dangling in clumps of darkness whenever she shut her eyes.

The man had pursued her ever since, clutching the book with the green cover. She had run past crossroads, turns in the road, and broken walls, beneath dark trees in the courtyards of ruined temples – only to come face to face with him. She would recognise him immediately, and run away.

But today, in her sleep, instead of running away, she stopped in her tracks. With darkness falling, she hastened back to the music school where the man had sat with his trousers unzipped, his diseased penis poking out, and the book with the green cover open before him. By now she knew that very few people possessed the kind of penis that could reach as far as a woman's desire, her womanhood. Then why be afraid? Why run away? She held the book open for the man. She turned the pages, displaying them to him, shaking the book in his face. 'Erect, erect ...' she screamed sharply. And the man shrank back, spittle trickling from his mouth as he stared blankly at his inanimate penis.

In her next dream, she prayed for every growing girl to sprout a tender green penis, like a vine, growing longer every day.

I had no idea where the lice came from. One day, I'd just started eating when something dropped from my head onto the plate. Squinting, I could make out waving limbs. I plucked it out of the food, placed it on the table and crushed it with my nail. It didn't bleed. A viscous fluid emerged – I couldn't go on with my meal.

As a child my hair was frequently infested. My mother would get tired of having to wage a year-round war against the lice. Sometimes her irritation was so great that she would insist on having my head shaved. But that didn't help. As soon as the hair grew back just a little I would come home from school with a head full of lice.

The elderly woman who worked as our maid loved killing lice. Whenever she had time on her hands she'd tell me, 'Come, let me clean it up.' One day my mother discovered that you could kill them by blasting them with a hairdryer. From then on, whenever I had lice, I had to blow dry after my bath for several days in succession. Both my mother and I were relieved. Because the insecticide was ruining our hair. Whenever I had an infestation, so did my mother – it was inevitable.

The last time I had lice was twenty years ago.

We'd been best friends for as long as I could remember. Our house stood cheek by jowl with theirs. We used to play together all the time.

This woman I called Kakima had come to our neighbourhood as a new bride. She was forever out on her veranda, munching on pickles or guavas. She'd spit the guava pulp out onto the floor. Whenever the young men passed by on their bicycles, she'd call out to them, smiling, inviting them to chat. She would giggle as she pretended to pummel their backs. My friend and I were walking past hand in hand one day when Kakima called us over. After some small talk she asked me jokingly, 'Why is your hair so brown and coarse? People with brown hair are very quarrelsome. Does that sound like you?' Kakima turned to my friend. 'Does she often pick fights with you?'

My friend glanced at me. 'Yes, we fight a lot, but we always make up …' she answered.

'You don't look like much like a fighter,' said Kakima.

'Why doesn't she?' I asked.

'Just take a look at her hair. Black, neat, beautiful. Not unkempt like yours.'

'Is that all there is to it?' my friend asked.

She seemed upset by what Kakima had said. But it was she with whom I felt angry.

It was getting dark. 'Let's go sit on the culvert for a bit,' I said.

'I know you're upset,' she said. 'Kakima is too smart for her own good. My mother says so too. You haven't done her any harm. What good did it do her to hurt you?'

I was silent.

'We'll never behave as badly as she has, all right?'

Sitting next to her on the culvert, I rested my head against hers. I knew that the lice were transferring from my hair to hers, one at a time. One, two, three, four …

Indeed, her hair was soon infested. Her scalp began to itch. Lice eggs were visible all the way to the tips of her long hair. Her mother also had thick, long hair. I kept telling her, 'Just put insecticide in your hair every night. It'll be fine.'

After a while her mother chopped off her hair. Then she chopped off her own hair too. Hand in hand, she and I watched all that hair of theirs being burnt to ashes … Then they began to apply the insecticide to their scalps.

That was the last time I had lice. I never allowed it to happen again. I took meticulous care of my hair, never letting my guard down. But now, after all this time, my head was infested again, and I had no idea how.

It was horrible. Granted, my head had been itching for a few days, but I hadn't paid it any attention. I couldn't figure out where the lice could have come from. I hadn't seen anyone since I came here. I had no friends or family to meet up with. No neighbours either. I didn't pay anyone a visit. I rarely used public transport, preferring to walk if I needed to go somewhere. I couldn't think of a woman whose head might have touched mine – lice are most often found in women's hair.

Had an old lice egg survived in my hair for two decades only to hatch now?

Not that there was such a need to fret. Anti-lice shampoo is readily available these days. That plus a hairdryer would kill all the lice, including the larvae.

I'd been thinking of going shopping in the evening. But I showed no sign of going. I managed five days of procrastination. The itching intensified.

Eventually I made it to the shop. The anti-lice shampoo glowed amidst all the other haircare brands. But, after taking a pensive look at it, I turned on my heels and walked out of the shop. On my way back to the flat, I came across a man squatting on the pavement, hawking all kinds of household goods. Nylon clotheslines, strainers, small baskets, hangers … among his wares, I spotted a small, thin comb for removing lice. I bought it.

I waited until around midnight, maybe even later, before I sat on the bed in my white skirt, positioning myself directly beneath the light, and ran the thin comb through my hair. The lice began to stream onto the skirt, showing up against the white fabric. And what fun – they scurried off this way and that. But none of them escaped – I killed them in droves. Sometimes I simply pinched them between my fingers and held them up instead of finishing them off.

Perhaps I didn't want to completely exterminate the lice. I plucked the rest out without killing them. And then I returned them to my hair. My days passed in anticipation. Somewhere on a distant roof, a mouth organ sounded deep into the night, to comfort some living being.

She was writing a letter. To whom? She was writing to time. She would put the letter in a bottle, seal its mouth, and throw it into the sea. Because she was planning to visit the seaside soon. In the letter she wrote, 'I don't know why I went there. Why I used to go back again and again. Or why I even thought of it in the first place. Why did I consider Shwetaketu and Babhravya wrong on matters of sexual choice? Why did I think Vatsyayana was ignorant? Why did I believe that the identity of an object should be sought in its insecurities? Why was I convinced that an object blooms by virtue of its own uncertainties? Why did I tell the man to take my internal clock into account? Why did I ask him to stop at those moments ... to stop ... to stop ...'

I didn't have the answer to any of these questions. All I knew was that no matter what I sought in life, all I got were 'relationships'.

Taking off her clothes, she called out to you. You shook your head no. You said, 'I want you on top this time.' There was something unfamiliar in your words that brought her up short. She was conflicted, unable to figure out what exactly you were after. That was when you repeated, 'Get on top of me. Get on top the way a man mounts a woman, and establish yourself. Find out for yourself how your masculinity is aroused in your being. See if you can discover the woman within the man lying beneath you.' You had already identified each of the insecurities that made her a 'woman'. Which was why you said, 'The set conditions for sex or for a relationship are not the same for men and women.' You said, 'Come out of yourself for once and take a man as a man.'

She mounted you then, conducting herself like a rider on a horse. Every time she leaned towards you she discovered the man hidden within herself – her hands on your chest tried to cup a pair of non-existent breasts, your lips appeared as pleasurable as a woman's. Weeping, she held you in her arms.

At that moment, all the doors and windows of a repressed sexuality were flung open. She became aware of the wind and the sunlight. She regarded your erect penis with deep affection. She felt tears welling up again, and allowed them to fall one by one into the lips of your penis, like individual strands of pubic hair. And she began to torment it. It trembled, made you tremble too, and an introspective, penetrating stream spurted from it. Which she had never observed as closely as she did now. Never looked at, never touched, never sniffed, never tasted. Her consciousness accepted this liquid. She drank the sperm.

She went back home, and, later that same day, wrote 'I know the taste of sperm! The juice from tender green shoots of wheat, sliced and grated ten days after being planted in soft earth, tastes exactly like sperm. Just as the beating heart of the wheat seedlings throbs in that juice, the spirit of life can be clearly discerned when drinking sperm. When the liquid slides down the tongue, its effervescence spreads all the way to the windpipe.' Dying without ever having known this extraordinary taste means failing as a woman. It is the duty of a man to help a woman experience this unique taste. This helping hand is known as love.

3

——————

'Do you now understand what your nation is?'

Yes. One day I woke up very early and went out onto the balcony ... the rain that had fallen overnight had washed the streets clean. The water dripping from the leaves was so clear that I wanted to open my mouth and drink it. That was when I saw a sanyasi walking along the road from the east.

That dawn, he passed along the pavement muttering incantations I couldn't hear, waking all of those who were sleeping there. He had a large bag slung over his shoulder – the young sanyasi carried it with ease. I expected him to take food, clothes and medicine out of this bag and distribute them amongst the pavement dwellers. But all he did was wake them up – he never offered them anything. There wasn't the slightest sign of kindness, love, affection or sympathy in his eyes – all they held was a steely, cruel rejection of every human expectation. They gave out a one-word invitation – 'Come.' If you felt it was impossible to

join him, no explanation would suffice – such was the
language of his eyes. No one joined him, only offered
their respects. That dawn, it was he whom I identified
as my nation.

Accusing others, complaining, using my heart to
sear another's heart, searing it with memory, using my
body to set theirs on fire – such activities had been
my main occupation for a long time now. Even the
previous day had been saturated with feelings of hurt.
Plants and trees have no front or back, but I still hadn't
been able to shake the feeling that they had turned
their faces away from me – that they had spread out
their branches and leaves in the opposite direction.
But this following dawn had turned out completely
different. I could sense no lingering grievances – a different emotion oozed out of me. All these plants and
trees felt like my fathers, my ancestors.

How had this happened? The wet black tree trunks
seemed to be dripping with love – just for me.

Late that afternoon I went for a walk by the river.
Near the ghat, I stopped, catching sight of the young
sanyasi from that morning. An elderly woman was
resting her head against his chest, weeping, and the
sight confused me. It felt as though I was seeing my
own future. How terribly tragic those sobs were – like
water flowing over marble.

I heard the sanyasi ask her, 'What have you done for your nation?'

The woman said, 'Have I given anything without seeking a price for it?'

The sanyasi said, 'There's still time. Your nation lies here on this side of the river. Beyond, there is only the river, flowing – without past, present or future, without demands. You have to choose one of the two …'

'I'll go to the other side,' said the woman.

'Then let me take you across,' said the sanyasi, escorting her down the steps. Overcoming my be-wilderment, I followed them. They got into a boat. But before I could take another step, I heard someone calling me. The voice was strange, but I felt sure that it was me they were calling. The voice floated up, pulsating with feeling – 'O Baula, Baula, Baula re … e … e … e, e Baula, Baula, Baula re … e … e … e …' – the call seemed intended to flip my perspective, changing my view of my life. Within it, a thousand intoxicating fruits burst at every moment, wrapping themselves around my existence. In it, I discovered an irresistible call to return – compressed layers of sound seemed to travel from the back of my head to the tips of my hair, penetrating my consciousness.

I left the dark ghat and climbed back to the road, seeking the source of this sound. As I walked, again came that cry I could get drunk on, 'Baula, Baula, Baula re … e … e … e!'

Eventually I had to stop, for my feet were entangled in weeds and vines. In front of me I saw a truck.

The truck had stood beneath the abandoned bridge for countless years – waiting to carry my corpse away, Baula. Soft tendrils wound around its tyres and up the wooden railings at the back, climbing all the way to the roof before descending to the headlights, its eyes. It had waited there for years, waiting for me to find it. It wanted me to remove the tendrils and kiss it, to start the engine and restore it to motion – but you've written such a song, Baula, that my death wish won't go away. It makes me want to turn into a vine and coil around this nation, this land, this river, this light and shade – to kneel in front of the sanyasi and admit that this nation has given me a great deal indeed.

This is the sanyasi who has no longer renounced everything. Now, he wishes for something of his own – after all this time, I have finally learned to identify him as my nation.

16

Earlier, not long after darkness had fallen, we sat on the long veranda outside the club. The large crystal lampshades shed a strange golden glow. I looked up, and my gaze settled on the blank white hoarding on a tall building in Chowringhee. A black bird flew in front of the white hoarding, and I gaped in astonishment. I tugged at your arm with such force that you spilled vodka onto your trousers. 'What's the matter?' you said. Excited, I said, 'Look, look at the bird flying away from the hoarding. I thought for a moment that it was part of an advertisement, and had come alive.'

'What on earth put such a strange notion into your head?'

'No idea. Maybe because the hoarding is so white, without any pictures or words, the bird seemed to be part of it.'

'Yes, maybe ... We do nothing in isolation – there's always a background, something to support a given action or thought. But I can't tell which is the backdrop here – the white hoarding or the bird.'

'But you know what, the whole scene was actually something I imagined. Which is why it brought me happiness, albeit only for a moment.'

You looked at me when I said this, and I smiled back at you.

Just then two dogs ran across the lawn of the club, emerging from the darkness. One black, the other red. The black dog rolled on the grass right in front of us.

There was nothing new in this scene. These dogs belonged to the club. They could be seen there every day, larking about. So I turned back to you and was about to say something when you signalled to me to look back at the dogs. Something flashed in your eyes. Something familiar – I'd seen it before, flashing in a man's eyes when he looked at a woman. Sometimes … rarely …

Overwhelmed, I looked back at the dogs. The red dog had collapsed on the grass, its legs folded beneath it. It appeared to be trembling. And the black dog sniffed audibly …

I was completely overcome by the sound of the black dog sniffing, accompanied by the red dog's soft, seductive yelps. I felt the blood course up from my toes to my head. You took my left hand with your right, interlaced our fingers, squeezed mine briefly and then pulled away. Your lips swelled. I examined you closely. In your trousers and long-sleeved silk shirt you looked like a spirited black steed – heated, thrilling, aroused. The collar of your shirt lay like a pointed dagger against your fair cheek. Desire gripped me. Almost inaudibly, you whispered, 'If you're the red one, I'll be the black.'

Lightning flashed in the monsoon sky. Startled, the red dog sprang to its feet and raced away. The black dog gave chase.

'Chasing …' you said. 'Chasing for pure sex. Only sex, nothing else.' You paused, looked into my eyes, at my hair, at my lips and breasts, then said, 'Imagine me chasing you like that.' My throat felt parched. I gulped. The dogs came racing back. As soon as the red dog slowed down the black one mounted her, and you and I forgot everything as we watched him trying to push himself inside.

Your breath against my face was impossibly heavy. My whole body throbbed. You called the waiter at once, 'The bill …' I sensed your urgency – I smelled you in the air.

Signing swiftly to pay for the vodka, your fingers grazed my hand before you stood up and strode to the portico. I followed. You seemed impatient, starting the engine before I'd even closed the door. Kolkata at 10 p.m. rushed past outside the windows. In the car, you touched your lips to mine, briefly, just once.

The only additional time we needed was to unlock all the padlocks and get to the bedroom. You turned on the air conditioner, put your glasses on the table, tossed your mobile phone onto the bed. As you stripped me of my clothes, hurrying to get everything off, I was unbuttoning your shirt. You still had your shirt on when I was only in my ... I stood there in nothing but the leopard-print panty, shielding my breasts with my arms. I seemed to be standing like that for hours. Then I saw that you were surprised, saw you shrink back in hatred. Your loathing transformed into rage, rage changed to disappointment, then disappointment gave way to tears. Weeping, you left the flat.

Much, much later, I collapsed onto the bed. Lying on my back, I tried to release all the tears I'd been making such a tremendous effort to suppress. No one could hear me, but I said the words anyway. 'Can we ever have pure sex again? Does it ever happen that way with human beings? Pure sex? The way it happened between the red dog and the black dog – effortlessly.'

The next day you told me, 'Happiness now is like the bird that flew out of the white hoarding – it may be real, or it may be only imagined, a trick of the eye – we don't really want to know.'

21

─────

The doctor confirmed that my blood count was suffi-
ciently high for the surgery to go ahead. But neither
he nor we had taken into account the other conditions
that needed to be filled. 10.2 per cent haemoglobin
is no guarantee of eligibility. We soon realised our
mistake. We learned that, among other things, one
of the most important requirements is a signature.
Ideally that of a close relative, though a friend or
well-wisher would also do. A name and address were
also required. Who were the nursing authorities to
summon if the patient needed something? Who, for
that matter, would take charge if the patient were
to die during the surgery? Someone had to sign, to
confirm that they were aware of the various risks, and
that they took the responsibility upon themselves.

Not that any of this was running through my mind
at the time. Nor through yours, perhaps. We went to
the nursing home early in the morning. The opera-
tion was scheduled for that same evening. As the final

stage in the admission procedure, they held the form out to you. Naturally, they assumed that you were my guardian. And you accepted the form without demur.

Midway through filling out the form you paused and looked at me. 'The risk bond has to be signed,' you said.

I felt a stab of doubt. 'What do we do?' I asked. 'Can you assume the risk?'

'Risk?' you repeated. 'If anyone's risking anything right now, it's me. But they want to know our relationship. "What is the relationship between the patient and the signatory?"'

My insides began to hollow out. 'Oh, "relationship" ...' I said.

'What is the relationship?'

'Don't you know?'

'No.'

'Neither do I.'

'What should I write?'

'Whatever you like. Or leave it, don't write anything. Never mind the surgery.'

Did I want to cry? Was I trying to cling to you purely for the sake of having someone, anyone, who could sign the bond? Did I grasp the helplessness – the danger, at times – of lacking anyone with whom I could be said to have a relationship? Did I desire recovery despite all this? Had I previously been aware that, in this world, every relationship is an existential matter – that relationships are necessary for one's very survival? That not even a dead body can do without them? Was I scanning the marble floor and white walls of the nursing home in search of a 'relationship', just in case I found one lying around? Was my faith renewed in a relationship of real weight and solidity, a relationship which could not be explained – a relationship strong enough to bear responsibility for the risk of death? That could welcome death with open arms? Did I need to put a name on a personal relationship – like a sound that is born in the mountains and echoes around those same peaks? I sat with my head bowed in shame, defeated. I had no relationship to claim, so there was nothing else for it but for me to leave. And yet, as it turned out, I didn't have to. On the form you wrote, 'I love this woman. And she loves me. Out of love she has given me her heart and her body. So her body is mine, her heart is mine. This means that whatever she needs, before or after the surgery, is my responsibility. The risk of the surgery is mine to bear. If, for some unfortunate reason, she dies during this surgery, I shall take her body and carry it away. In addition to my address and phone number given below, please find attached some documents which can act as proof of address …'

9

The rain starts in the afternoon. And lasts until evening. From evening until morning, through afternoon and evening again – and still it does not stop. It falls continuously. In the early hours of the morning it turns torrential – by dawn it is evident that the entire city is submerged.

I see all the family's things being swept away in the water. The lid of the wooden packing box in which they store their belongings is floating away. As are their plastic sheets, glasses and plates. They keep falling on their faces as they try to chase after them, splashing and laughing riotously. I lean over the railing to try and get a better look, but cannot spot the two children anywhere. I go back out to the balcony several times that day. Much later, the young woman appears below, the water now up to her waist. 'Where are your children?' I ask.

She raises her arm and points, but I cannot see where. 'Where are they?' I repeat.

'I've left them over there, out of the reach of the water.'

This worries me. 'Who's with them?'

'No one.'

'What! What if the little one falls in …'

She turns away without answering and begins to wade through the water, hurling abuse, possibly directed at her husband. 'Couldn't you get the sheets out of the water in time, you asshole?' She spits twice into the same water she is wading through.

Suppressing my revulsion, I say, 'Leave your daughters near the staircase. I'll bring them upstairs. Take them back when the water goes down.'

This time she is genuinely surprised, and, craning her neck upwards, asks, 'What did you say?'

'I said, bring your daughters here …' Throwing me a strange glance, she wades away.

She comes back a little later, splashing through the water with her babies in her arms. 'Take this one,' she says, 'the other can't do without my breast milk …'

The durwan and drivers clustered around the gate regard me with astonishment when I appear at the bottom of the stairs and collect the naked baby. Just a moment ago they were in an uproar over the water in the basement.

The first thing I do when I get back upstairs is call you to tell you what I've done. 'Bad idea,' you say, clearly annoyed. 'It's just not done. Experimenting with human beings? You'll regret it. Although, why not try it out – at least then you'll realise you've had it wrong. It's always best to learn from your own mistakes …'

I bathe the child and feed her. I teach her to use the toilet, urinating in front of her to demonstrate. I trim her wild hair with a pair of scissors, and drape my chunni around her like a sari, whereupon she walks up to the mirror and stands there shyly, keeping her eyes on the floor. After much coaxing she looks up at me.

The water ebbs away the next day – unlike my boldness. With a look of terror, your man tells me, 'Sahib will give us hell, Behenji, he'll accuse us of not looking after you …'

'Don't worry,' I comfort him, 'you can go now. I've informed him of everything.' A couple of days pass. I buy clothes, shoes, baby cream and baby soap. I am growing very fond of her. Her large eyes, dark pouting lips and snub nose work their magic on me, never failing to calm me down. I keep glancing over at her, expecting her to say something.

But she doesn't. She communicates solely through gestures. Even the manner in which she looks for her mother is subtle. She goes out onto the balcony, either spots her mother and blushes or, if the woman is nowhere to be seen, lowers her eyes and picks at her nails, then comes away.

My hopes rise with every passing day. One day she eats some milk and cornflakes with a spoon. Another day, she comes to fetch me when the phone rings. Even you become accustomed to asking after her. While her parents no longer bother to enquire …

I dress her in her best frock the day you come round. She stands up as soon you arrive – yes, she recognises you – she used to see you visit this building when she lived on the pavement – yes, she wobbles towards you – and then stands in front of you – and I see her hold out her upturned palm, saying, 'I haven't eaten today …'

I return her the next afternoon. 'Let me take you to your mother,' I tell her.

I don't know why I insist upon taking the staircase instead of the lift, holding her hand all the way. Maybe all of my actions have simply been in order to compose these moments when I would send her back – taking the stairs is a way of prolonging them, of milking my own unhappiness.

With each step down, she shakes her head. One step down, one shake of the head. Another step, another shake. She's trying to say that she doesn't want to go – that she would rather stay. She doesn't know what it means to stay, any more than what it means to go, but, both understanding and not, she protests. A silent, unobtrusive 'no'. She goes down the stairs and, with each shake of her head a 'no' …

Eventually she came across the wall of death, in one of the bathrooms at the other end of the flat. She'd just happened to venture into the bathroom, all the walls of which were covered in black tiles. The floor and basin table were black granite. The commode and sink were black. Even the fittings. The windowpanes and lampshades too – everything was black. Only the space on the wall above the sink, which should have held a large mirror, was not. There, the bricks were showing. They were a dusty grey, covered in cobwebs, which had spiders in them.

She paused, wondering. She knew that there would be a bedroom on the other side of the wall. She knew that the wall was only four or five inches thick. She knew that the wall was solid. But still she wondered. She stifled the sigh that rose up in her, for she knew that this was the wall of death, on this side of which she lived her fearful life.

Standing before the wall, she felt afraid and wanted to plug the gap in it, but her mōn dissuaded her. 'You've spent all your life running away from death,' it told her, 'now, try to understand it.'

In an attempt to understand death, she brought her face close to the gap in the wall and whistled. She whistled. And as she whistled she realised that the sounds were multiplying – from one to two, two to four, four to many more – and rustling out from inside the wall. Rustling. This made her unhappy, so, to try and shake the feeling, she returned to the part of the flat she normally used, leaving the door to that bathroom open.

Many, many years ago, when she had approached a body eager for death, her guardian had instructed her to move away. 'Get back,' the guardian had said, 'if you don't want fear to possess you.'

After that, she had turned her back on so many deaths, fleeing in the opposite direction as instructed by some unseen figure. Running away was all she had ever done. This life was nothing but a constant flight from death, her pursuer. Survival was nothing more than keeping death at bay. She had seen death lurking somewhere near fear. It could not be discerned in isolation – as something separate, pure and complete. Although what happened every minute, every second,

on earth was caused by 'death', death had no existence of its own. Fear was the key.

The next day, she went for a swim. The days
were getting colder. The pool was deserted at that
hour, which made it the best time to visit. It was
late evening. The darkness was deeper in the dense
greenery surrounding the pool. The bright lights
were still on, turning the water nearest her a liquid
gold. But the far end of the pool was dark.

She slipped into the water and swam to the far end,
where she began to float on her stomach. She was
looking down at twelve feet of water. 'Think of this as
death,' she told herself. 'Feel this twelve foot depth of
death.' No sight, no sound, penetrated her consciousness. She wasn't even breathing – her mind detached
itself and drifted down. She couldn't believe that she'd
already lived an entire life; her mind began to shed
everything one by one – consciousness, memories,
smells, sights, tastes, desires, all passed from her into
the water. She passed beyond emptiness.

Even underwater she could sense the growing
light, spreading from some secret sunrise. Thereafter!
A little boy broke into peals of laughter as a poet rose
from the water. She addressed him thus: 'Baula!' Her
voice burst out of her with a stream of bubbles. She
tried to accept all of this as death.

Back home, she stood before the wall of death, on this side of which lay her fear, her survival, her own death, everything – while on the other side nothing existed, and nothing ever had.

17

I wanted you to tell me about her, over and over again. As I listened, I experienced a certain sensation that I could not explain. It was a mixture of jealousy, anger, hatred, curiosity, and even pity. I felt anguish, too, and physical pain. Sometimes my heart brimmed over with sympathy; I seemed to become 'her'. In my own way.

You couldn't quite figure out what I wanted at such moments. You felt helpless to begin with. You looked deep into my eyes, hoping to discover my real intentions. Your eyes appeared slightly glazed. Then you began to tell me about her, both under-standing and not, and your pupils gradually regained their blackness. The truth of your relationship with her seemed not to have altered. If anything, it had deepened. You drifted back to the old days, sinking into them gradually, until you were no longer seeing me.

'I have no idea what happened to her that last day.' Your voice was helpless, despairing. 'When I came to this flat I found her painting a mural across the entire wall. I had no idea when she'd found the time to obtain all the paints and brushes. She'd only been here for a couple of months. She looked lovely, in a short pink skirt and a white blouse. Her face showed clear signs of fatigue. I might have mistaken her for a schoolgirl had those breasts so familiar to me not been conspicuously pert, had I not noticed the shapely calves and knees – which had nothing girlish about them, they were every inch a woman's – and the thighs that had accommodated men's tears. She looked beautiful. Her hair was gathered at her neck. The paintbrushes were tucked into her waist. Pots of paint were scattered over the floor. She'd been painting both sitting and standing, shifting the chair around as needed. My regret over the disfigured wall was fleeting, and I began to enjoy the scene. The painting gradually came to life on the enormous wall.

'She painted a life-sized couple – man and woman – on the huge blank canvas of the wall. The couple were making love, in an unusual pose. Strangely, the impression was one of both extreme sexuality and total detachment. As though she was trying to say that sex is a form of self-discovery, and that the immediate aftermath involves tearing oneself away at the very moment of this discovery. Because you're constantly striving to get to that someone else inside you – and no sooner has sex afforded you that sensation than it isolates you, like the seed spat out by the exploding fruit. This post-coital loneliness is the root of all despair. You desire to be conjoined, it's all you want – you cannot ask for anything more divine. To be joined with someone within you – this is the only demand that remains constant throughout a human being's life. We eat, sleep, engage in conversation, but a part of our minds remains submerged in sex all the while – there, sex is constantly being enacted, a penis enters a vagina, touches its soft muscles, life touches life, returns, goes back, returns again, goes back again …

'As she painted she became increasingly aroused, and kept inviting me to make love to her. So I did. She screamed as she climaxed, "I love it, I love it," so loud it made the walls shake. At one point our skin seemed to fuse together.

'It was late at night by the time she was done with the painting. That was the first time I stayed over so late. I stayed, I was able to stay, because all the doubts in my mind had been extinguished by then. I'd decided to tell everyone about her. My elderly mother, my children, my siblings. Everyone. And I'd decided to tell her, ten days later, on her birthday – to tell her what she'd already told me, over and over again as she clung to my arm. I would say the words and watch the surprise jump into her eyes. She would either burst into tears or stare at me in silence, but then she would jump up and cry out, "We'll get married? We'll get married? Will there be music all day and all night?"

'It was around eleven at night, maybe a little later. I didn't want to separate our fused skin. But I had to leave. I ran my tongue over her naked lips in a final kiss. I wanted to tell her there and then, "I'm ready," to let her know all of my plans. There had been one other time in my life when I didn't get around to saying "I love you." In that instance, the woman left me before I could make up my mind to tell her. Despite this, I still wanted to wait the extra ten days this time. I pressed her hand lightly in lieu of a goodbye, but she gripped my hand and wouldn't let go. She just looked at me, a faint smile on her lips. Then she said, "Everyone at home wants me to go back. They're not angry with me any more. On the contrary, they're worried. I'm leaving tomorrow. I've agreed to get married. That same man is waiting for me, the one who was the reason I left. I left home to come here and wait for your decision. Such a chain of waiting. He's been waiting for me, I've been waiting for you. Let this chain break now. My wedding preparations will begin as soon as I return. There's very little time. Earlier, I was afraid – I'd already given you all I had. What did I have left to offer, how could I start a life with someone else? But I've overcome that fear now – I can take all that I got from you away with me, and offer it to someone else. Everything you've taught me – to give and take with all that one has – and you've taught me so much physically, too, that I know I can make any man happy now. Whoever ends up as my companion will be satisfied, will always turn to me … unless … "

"'Unless …?" I asked.

"'Unless you ever recognise me after today.'"

I hid my face in my hands.

'She said, "Even if we do happen to meet, let there be no flash of recognition in your eyes. Let the portion of your heart in which I exist die this very moment. Let us free ourselves from this bond as far as is possible."

'I never tried to find out what happened after that. Only after several months had passed did I go back to the flat. That was when I had the wall painted over, in a deliberately deep shade. But you tell me that the image can be seen through the paint, that the figures come alive and make love in a frenzy. I cannot accept this as the truth. Because she has left forever, beyond a doubt she has left – like the dead, she cannot return your love or make someone love her …'

When I heard you say these last words, I wept. Weeping, I returned to this flat. After being chastised by sorrow in its real form, I yearned for you. I wanted to wipe your sorrowful face and draw it to my breast.

Lying in bed, I thought of you. I thought of your heart. I thought of your thighs and your shins, your arms and your embrace. But I couldn't picture myself at your side. Instead, I found her taking my place. Naked, poised, eager. You drew together hungrily. I watched your lovemaking. And pleasure coursed through my body. Thinking of you, I came, shouting 'I love it, I love it.'

Then, I couldn't tell whether it was I who said it or she: 'We will be married one day, one day there will be music all day and night. Having played all day and night, the music will stop of its own accord. It will stop … and gasp …'

She had consigned the panty to the flames. She had burned her attachment to her life as a woman. As a result, she was exhausted. Exhausted, she had wandered to this place …

Over there, whores were lined up like a row of the goddess Durga's idols. Meanwhile, on this side, the goddess Kali, full of possibilities, might awaken at any moment.

In between was the Ganga – or was it just a canal of loathsome black bilge?

The steps of the ghat led down to the water on both sides. A wooden boat to ferry people across was moored to the opposite bank. On this one, a wooden tray was being washed in the diseased water.

She stood on the broad steps of the ghat. Blue aparajita flowers – clitoria – were scattered near her feet. A mangy dog had been following her for some time. It was eleven at night, and a philanthropist was distributing bread to beggars. The beggars were clamouring for more. Though actually, they had no expectations. No expectations of the temple in which they stood, no expectations of the country in which they lived.

A blind beggar was playing his castanets without let-up. He seemed to have appeared before mankind in this form for centuries, though no one had recognised him. His tragic music had made one of them part with a rupee or two – the only one who had identified the gift he had given them in return. The elderly priest kept ringing the temple bell. He was eager to make a few more sacrifices to the goddess.

A woman wandered about alone, reciting Radha's speech to Krishna, the illicit lover she called by another name: 'I beg of you, Shyam,' she said, 'I beg of you, even if I, Radharani, die, don't forsake me in the darkness. If you do, I shall set up my own pyre by the Yamuna and burn myself to death. Wherever you may be, the smoke from the pyre will sting your eyes, wherever you may be, your heart of stone will dissolve in tears.'

She was already feeling overwhelmed when a stooped old woman whispered into her ear, 'The bitch usually whores around day and night. It's just once a month when she's indisposed that she pretends to be Radha.'

Neither the prostitute nor the goddess – there was no one who could grant her forgiveness. Both were incomplete entities in her life. It was no use hanging around on the bank of the Ganga. She would go back now. Go back and stab herself in the vagina ... stab herself over and over ... she would stab herself in the vagina until it died.

SAHANA, OR SHAMIM

Even in the aftermath of 9/11, Sahana regular-
ly bought fish. Also after the Godhra incident in
her own country. Taking advantage of Paramesh's
absence, overcoming her hesitation, she never missed
a single opportunity to buy fish. So many people were
dying every day in Kashmir, America was tearing
Iraq to pieces. Militants nurtured by the ISI were
taking shelter in Bangladesh, even Kolkata wasn't safe
any more. The air was thick with rumours, you felt
afraid to step out of your home, being in a crowd was
uncomfortable, the cinema-hall made you claustro-
phobic – but still, skirting all these truths, Sahana had
carried on buying fish. When she entered the market,
she looked around for a bit, then casually approached
the area where the fish was sold. She indicated the
one she wanted, paid for it, put it in her shopping bag
and went home. All with her mouth clamped shut.
Cautiously. Even rinsing the fillets made her hands
shake.

It happened every time – from the moment of the transaction, through carrying her purchase home in her oversized shopping bag, gingerly rinsing the fillets, gathering the scales and other scraps with an unerring hand, only stopping when she threw these out of the window of her high-rise apartment, into the grounds of the British bungalow next door. Her hands shook, she found it difficult to breathe, her head reeled!

And how self-flagellating the act of frying the fish was. Constantly she felt as though Paramesh were standing next to her, crying, 'Flesh, flesh!' She started in alarm every now and then, certain that her fear would lead to an accident. Her own carelessness would end in her burning to death. The stench of her roasting flesh would mingle with the savour of fried fish.

But death would not bring deliverance. The forensic report would specify that she had been frying fish when she went up in flames. Paramesh's heart would no longer harbour the detached mix of respect and love that people customarily felt for the dead. If there were any photographs of her in the flat, he would throw them away, damning her as a traitor. And hate her as long as he lived.

All of this was in Sahana's mind as she cooked the fish. She usually felt overwhelmed when she was done with the cooking. Unable to control herself, she ate the fish with rice, experiencing an acute sense of satisfaction. But as soon as she had eaten, she began to pant. Fear seized her, weighing her down like a huge slab of stone. She didn't even pause to blink till she had washed and scoured the utensils, the ladles, the table, the oven – the entire kitchen, in fact – frantically, until they gleamed. She sprayed freshener in every room, poured phenyl into the sink. Making sure not to miss a single one, she put the bones in a polythene packet and tossed them out of the window, watching them land among next door's fig trees. She poured soap on her hands, gargled with mouthwash, shampooed her hair – she showered! She showered!

Not a trace of the smell remained. Still she gave each room one more blast with the freshener and sniffed the palms of both hands. Sometimes, unable to handle such anxiety, Sahana pounded garlic into a paste and fried it in oil. All other smells were certain to be smothered.

But the situation had not been remotely like this when they first met and exchanged mōn. Fish had not seemed a significant issue during those early days of their romance. Sahana had never in the least felt that in linking her life to Paramesh's she was treading the path of sacrifice. She had accepted the whole thing without protest. Although she realised now that she had indeed wanted to protest – but simply hadn't been able.

'I'm vegetarian,' Paramesh had told her. 'You mustn't eat anything non-vegetarian at home.'

'What about elsewhere?' she had asked.

Paramesh was silent for a couple of seconds, then shrugged.

'I don't mind chicken. But as for fish, you'll have to give it up completely, at home or anywhere else. I simply cannot tolerate the smell of fish, Sahana. I throw up on the spot. It makes me so sick, there's been occasions when I've actually had to be hospitalised. I hate fish. Moreover, Sahana, I could never dream of kissing or making love to someone who eats fish. I can't enter someone who is, in whichever sense, fishy.'

Waggling the middle finger of his left hand at her, Paramesh had made sure that she understood all of what he meant by 'fishy'. 'So you have to give it up.'

By that point, Sahana had already fallen in love with Paramesh. If it had been only love, things might have been different, but she had also become psychologically dependent on him. She had realised that she would have to give up fish if she wanted to keep

Paramesh. There had been nothing else for it but to uproot the very desire for fish from her heart, and in fact this had been effortless. She simply trained her sights on all the other foods that existed in the world. Not a single flake of fish passed her lips in two whole years. Then the taste of it possessed her again.

And she began to eat fish in secret, and to fear Paramesh. For she was only too aware that if Paramesh came to know, their relationship would end. Alternatively, a conflict would erupt, a very familiar kind of conflict. The more Sahana began to fear Paramesh, the more she began to loathe him too. Hatred. Or, one could say that the more she became aware of Paramesh's abhorrence for fish and those who eat it, the more determined she became to retaliate with a proportionate degree of abhorrence for those who did not. She seemed to feel a certain responsibility to do this. Her growing self-awareness provided ammunition for her opposition to, and dis-illusionment about, Paramesh.

'Those who eat fish and those who don't are poles apart, separated by a deep gulf of mutual contempt.' Sahana grew deeply emotional about fish, and would argue, though with trepidation, 'Why should I be deprived of fish, Paramesh, just because you don't enjoy it, just because you can't stand the smell? Why should your behaviour dictate mine? I'm not you, I'm my own person, separate and distinct. That isn't going to change. Isn't it you that's mistaken, Param?'

Paramesh became furious, lecturing her on total surrender. 'Even if I'm wrong,' he replied, 'I expect unquestioning submission from you in this regard. Remember that there is no alternative if this relationship is to be maintained in its most peaceful possible state. Or else, as you know, terrible things might happen, and you'd better not blame me when they do.'

Sahana's former lover Manish returned to her life at this precise juncture. Because hate spirals upwards, its root causes overshadowed by its object's increasing centrality, Sahana entered into an illicit relationship with Manish for no particular reason, simply out of loathing for Paramesh.

One evening, at a small party at a friend's house, Paramesh started railing against eating meat and fish. 'The most extreme form of enjoying meat is cannibalism,' he declared. 'Human flesh is the most delicious of all!'

Sahana wept buckets that evening, sitting on the toilet in the friend's house. Finally, she ground her teeth – 'So it's hatred? So much hatred?' On the way home Paramesh's face appeared to be composed of nothing but a glutinous green substance. The next day she not only cooked some fish, she ate it in Manish's arms. Then, drawing strength from ultimate hatred for the first time in her life, she let Manish have her. But she could see that this hatred was working in its entirety on her and her alone. Since Paramesh could perceive nothing of it, since he had no inkling of this nightmarish loathing, the only person who had to suffer from it was Sahana herself. Poor Sahana! Not only was she the one doing the hating, she was also the one feeling its impact. Just like cheating – as long as the person being cheated on remains ignorant of their deception, the burden is borne entirely by the one doing the cheating. And again, the moment it all comes to light, technically speaking there's no more deception. And yet the person who had done the cheating continues to bear the entire burden, as before! In other words, people can cheat, but can never be cheated – it really was entirely one-sided.

In the same way, Sahana cheated Paramesh, but Paramesh wasn't cheated. Sahana hated, but Paramesh did not feel himself to be the object of hatred. Sahana remained perpetually drenched in her own loathing. Yet whenever Paramesh wanted to be intimate with her, at whatever time of day or night, he smelt straw-berry, gulabjamun or mint on her breath. He was able to kiss her fervently, his body completely relaxed. He could say, 'Have you stopped loving me, Sana? Why else would your mouth be so cold?'

At the same time, when she came to cook the fish she had bought, Sahana would frequently discover that it was rotten. Completely putrefied! During sex with Manish she would discover that she didn't want him, while with Paramesh she suffered from guilt, disquiet and fear – with hatred filling the rest of her hours. This unspoken, inarticulate hatred progressively crossed the limits of forbidden pleasure, rotting just like stale fish. Yet Sahana could not simply pick out the scales and bones and throw them away. She could not forget that she and Paramesh were repulsively unalike.

Paramesh had been in London on 7/7. Sahana hadn't switched her TV on that morning, so she didn't know anything about the explosions till Pubali called her in the afternoon.

Frantic, she tried to call Paramesh on his mobile. But a pre-recorded voice kept informing her that 'the subscriber is out of reach at this moment ...'

Their friends came to the house one by one. Manish, Pubali, Tushar, Vasundhara. Each of them tried through their own means to get some information about Paramesh. But evening stretched into night and there was still no news, neither from Paramesh nor of him.

Despite their collective efforts, Sahana's friends failed to calm her down. Her behaviour was completely out of control. Although they could make out her words, none of them could understand what she meant by them.

'My hatred has killed Paramesh,' Sahana was shrieking, in tears, 'my continuous hatred. Was it necessary to hate him so much?'

The day passed in a whirl. Paramesh did not return. A week later Sahana boarded a flight to London, along with her sister and brother-in-law. And returned without Paramesh.

There was no trace of Paramesh anywhere. No sign. There was no way to tell whether he was dead or alive.

A couple of months later Manish visited Sahana. She seized his arm. 'I'm converting, Manish,' she told him. 'I'm going to become a Muslim.'

Manish was speechless. If Sahana's decision was related to her grief over Paramesh, he couldn't fathom how.

'Paramesh used to talk of complete submission, Manish,' Sahana continued.

'We cannot live together until you become me,' he would say. 'I could say the same to you, Param, I would snap back at him.'

'But he would shake his head. Total submission means unquestioning surrender, he would say. Where there is no scope for asking questions. Where questions don't even exist.'

'Now that I don't know whether Paramesh will ever come back, there's only one way to perform the total submission he wanted. Only one. In a couple of days a senior Muslim priest will convert me. My name will be Shamim.'

Possibly understanding some of what Sahana was getting at, Manish brushed a few strands of hair from her face. 'Is there no other way, Sahana?' he asked.

'No, Manish, there isn't. There's no shortcut. No room for bargaining. I cannot become you with anything less than this. All other efforts would be in vain. This is what complete submission means, Manish. When Paramesh comes back he will realise that, although it took time, I'm now able to accept him with my whole heart.'

Don't raise any questions about this story, reader. Before you can, I would like to remind you that this is a story of unquestioning surrender.

This edition first published in the United Kingdom by Tilted Axis Press
in 2016, by arrangement with Penguin Books India.

tiltedaxispress.com

First published in Bengali as *Panty O Annyano Galpo* by Ananda Publishers,
Kolkata, 2006.
First published in English by Penguin Books India, 2014.

ISBN (paperback)   9781911284000
ISBN (ebook)   9781911284017

A catalogue record for this book is available from the British Library.

Edited by Deborah Smith
Copy-edited by Christopher Riley
Typesetting and ebook production by Simon Collinson
Printed and bound by CPI Group (UK) Ltd, Croydon, CR0 4YY

Supported by the National Lottery through Arts Council England.

ABOUT TILTED AXIS PRESS

Founded in 2015 and based in south London, Tilted Axis is a not-for-profit press on a mission to shake up contemporary international literature.

Tilted Axis publishes the books that might not otherwise make it into English, for the very reasons that make them exciting to us – artistic originality, radical vision, the sense that here is something new.

Tilting the axis of world literature from the centre to the margins allows us to challenge that very division. These margins are spaces of compelling innovation, where multiple traditions spark new forms and translation plays a crucial role.

As part of carving out a new direction in the publishing industry, Tilted Axis is also dedicated to improving access. We're proud to pay our translators the proper rate, and to operate without unpaid interns.

We hope you find this fantastic book as thrilling and beguiling as we do, and if you do, we'd love to know.

tiltedaxispress.com
@TiltedAxisPress